MR. HAPPY

by Roger Hargreaves

EGMONT

On the other side of the world, where the sun shines hotter than here, and where the trees are a hundred feet tall, there is a country called Happyland.

As you might very well expect, everybody who lives in Happyland is as happy as the day is long.

Wherever you go, you see smiling faces all around.

It's such a happy place that even the flowers seem to smile in Happyland.

And, as well as all the people being happy, all the animals in Happyland are happy, too.

If you've never seen a mouse smile, or a cat, or a dog, or even a worm – go to Happyland!

This is a story about someone who lived there who happened to be called Mr Happy.

Mr Happy was fat and round, and happy!

He lived in a small cottage beside a lake at the foot of a mountain and close to a wood in Happyland.

One day, while Mr Happy was out walking through the tall trees in those woods near his home, he came across something which was really rather extraordinary.

There in the trunk of one of the very tall trees was a door.

Not a very large door, but nevertheless a door. Certainly a door. A small, narrow, yellow door.

Definitely a door!

"I wonder who lives here?" thought Mr Happy to himself, and he turned the handle of that small, narrow, yellow door.

The door wasn't locked and it swung open quite easily.

Just inside the small, narrow, yellow door was a small, narrow, winding staircase, leading downwards.

Mr Happy squeezed his rather large body through the rather thin doorway and began to walk down the stairs.

The stairs went round and round and down and down and round and down and down and round.

Eventually, after a long time, Mr Happy reached the bottom of the staircase.

He looked around and saw, there in front of him, another small, narrow door. But this one was red.

Mr Happy knocked at the door.

"Who's there?" said a voice. A sad, squeaky sort of a voice. "Who's there?"

Mr Happy pushed open the red door slowly, and there, sitting on a stool, was somebody who looked exactly like Mr Happy, except that he didn't look happy at all.

In fact he looked downright miserable.

"Hello," said Mr Happy. "I'm Mr Happy."

"Oh, are you indeed?" sniffed the person who looked like Mr Happy but wasn't. "Well, my name is Mr Miserable, and I'm the most miserable person in the world."

"Why are you so miserable?" asked Mr Happy.

"Because I am," replied Mr Miserable.

"How would you like to be happy like me?" asked Mr Happy.

"I'd give anything to be happy," said Mr Miserable. "But I'm so miserable I don't think I could ever be happy," he added miserably.

Mr Happy made up his mind quickly. "Follow me," he said.

"Where to?" asked Mr Miserable.

"Don't argue," said Mr Happy, and he went out through the small, narrow, red door.

Mr Miserable hesitated, and then followed.

Up and up the winding staircase they went. Up and up and round and round and up and round and round and up until they came out into the wood.

"Follow me," said Mr Happy again, and they both set off through the wood back to Mr Happy's cottage.

Mr Miserable stayed in Mr Happy's cottage for quite some time. And during that time the most remarkable thing happened.

Because he was living in Happyland, Mr Miserable, ever so slowly, stopped being miserable and started to be happy.

His mouth stopped turning down at the corners.

And, ever so slowly, it started turning up at the corners.

And eventually, Mr Miserable did something that he'd never done in the whole of his life.

He smiled!

And then he chuckled, which turned into a giggle, which became a laugh. A big booming hearty huge giant large enormous laugh.

And Mr Happy was so surprised that he started to laugh as well. And both of them laughed and laughed.

They laughed until their sides hurt and their eyes watered.

Mr Miserable and Mr Happy laughed and laughed and laughed and laughed.

They went outside and still they laughed.

And because they were laughing so much, everybody who saw them started laughing as well. Even the birds in the trees started to laugh at the thought of somebody called Mr Miserable who just couldn't stop laughing.

And that's really the end of the story, except to say that if you ever feel as miserable as Mr Miserable used to, you know exactly what to do, don't you?

Just turn your mouth up at the corners.

Go on!